Author/CEO: Darrell King
COO/Marketing Mngr.: Elbert Jones Jr.
by

KJ Publications, Inc.
www.kjpublications.com
"The Evolution Of Street"

1

Michelle "Meeka" Fontaine was sitting in the waiting room, biting her fingernail as she broke it with her teeth, a few inches with every bite. She dragged her legs forward, her eyes drooping over to the expensive boot on the leg of the six foot one blonde model sitting next to her. The model chewed her gum nonchalantly. Meeka's gaze returned to her own Zulu army green ankle boots, and she chewed harder on her nails. If a stethoscope was placed on her chest at that exact moment, she was certain it would explode from the incessant thumping. Her eyes had not stopped peering at the model as she tried to estimate the price tag of all she was wearing. A hundred dollar teak and purple Versace blouse on a Neiman Marcus ankle skinny jeans, and a purple Betty Studded Saint Laurent ankle boots. She could mentally calculate everything to be close to two thousand dollars, which was about what she lived on for a month.

"Miss Fontaine," the secretary called out in a tone that sounded too burly to belong to a woman of her size.

Meeka jumped to her feet. "Yeah, that's me!" she exclaimed and walked closer.

"Mr. Young will see you now," she announced and buzzed the door open for her. Meeka smiled at her and pushed the door open. She took one last look at the girl she had left behind, and she could see she was unhappy that she got in before her. Meeka scowled at her before shutting the door behind her.

The big smile playing on Meeka's face as she turned to face the big man sitting behind the gigantic polished wooden table was in huge contrast to the murdering look she had thrown at the girl before she locked the door. She stood a few meters away from the table so that the man could have a clear view of her nice legs and her thighs. She had intentionally decided to reveal them to the man now in front of her. She waited, watching the man's eyes roam around her till he caught himself.

"Oh! You're here!" he exclaimed as though he had been staring at someone else's legs. "You can take your seat – if you want," he offered hoping she'd decline.

"Thank you, Mr. Young," she said and covered the distance between her and the four-legged cushioned seat in two strides. "I'm really glad to be here Mr. Young," she said and gave him another big smile. She had always known how to win people over with her smile. It was her biggest weapon, and she was prepared to murder Jonathan Young with the peering white teeth underneath the pouty pink lush lips.

"Well Miss Fontaine, we're glad to have you here too," he answered as his eyes were now resting on her frontal. He flipped through her papers with as much concentration as he gave to Willie, the janitor, who always knocked on his window for a Jackson every evening.

Meeka also noticed his lengthened gaze on her chest. She inched forward, revealing more cleavage before pushing herself back into her seat.

"I've gone through your documents already, and we'll be glad to have you here. I am sure you will get used to the crowd in no time. Your latent talents will surely be brought to light here Miss Fontaine," he smiled at her and stood up signaling the end of the interview.

"I'm sorry. That's all?" Meeka asked as she also stood to her feet gazing at him with a puzzled look lining her face.

"Yes. That would be all. You should resume work tomorrow," Jonathan replied. "Once you're in, come see me first, and I'll hand you over to Old Johnny."

"Thank you, Mr. Young. I will put my best into this job." Meeka smiled at the man once again before walking out of the door.

****

"Meeka, this is Jared Johnson, he will tutor you on all you need to know to catch up with what is needed of you daily. You do all he tells you to do and at the end of the day you report back to him," Jonathan Young dished out the information she needed, and as he was about to leave, he turned back and added, "Or you can just call him Old Johnny like the rest of us do – I'm sure he'd prefer that." Jonathan burst into a fit of laughter and walked away leaving her alone with her new boss, kind of.

"He's right though, I'd prefer it if you called me Old Johnny," Jared said and smiled at her. The first place he took her to was the coffee room. It was just seven-fifty in the morning, but it looked like the Starbucks on 43rd& Broadway. "This is our social ground – this is where it all happens, so be prepared to spend a lot of time here." Jared's words registered in her mind.

She nodded. "Got that." He took her around the building, introducing her to everyone in the different departments and when they were done greeting most of the staff, he led her back to her cubicle. He came to her later in the day with a file which he collected at the end of work.

"How was your first day?" Jonathan bumped up behind her as she was packing her bag set to leave.

"It was okay Mr. Young. Jare --- Old Johnny was really helpful," she answered.

"Come on, just call me Jonathan – that's what everyone calls me," he said. "And don't worry, you'll get used to calling him, Old Johnny. It wasn't easy for any of us," he smiled.

"Thank you," Meeka replied and pushed herself out of her chair. "I guess you're also closed for the day?"

"Yeah, technically but I still have to wait a little bit. I'm supposed to be present for a meeting the board is scheduled to have with the players later this evening," Jonathan replied with a tinge of disappointment in his voice.

"Oh," Meeka replied curtly.

"Well, you could still come out to party. We do a lot of partying, and there's always enough room for everyone. The guys will be glad to meet the new intern." Jonathan glared at her with heavy pleading eyes. He pouted his lips at her jokingly.

"Okay. I'll come," Meeka agreed, laughing.

"I'll text you the address." Jonathan smiled and went on his own way. Meeka walked the rest of the hallway beaming with smiles. She had always imagined herself with the boys, hoops around their necks, but she never thought she would one day party with them. Her smile soon turned into laughter as she thought of what her roommate was going to say.

"Who cares, she can be a total dickhead most times," Meeka hissed as she hopped into a taxi headed for her apartment.

"Hey Meeka, Come see this -" Laura called her as soon as she opened the door to the apartment. "– I can't fucking believe this guy went ahead with it. He freaking did it!" she exclaimed, as her eyes remained on the new iPhone 8 she just bought. Meeka grumbled and dragged her feet to join Laura on the cushion. It was either she gave Laura the attention she wanted now, or she would have to give it to her in bits, and she can testify that the latter was hell.

"Who are you talking about?" Meeka asked and stretched her feet to rest on the polished wooden center table.

"Who else if not Tyrone Dub. The guy proposed to Emilia Clark. Can you believe that?" The fire burning in her eyes was not doing much justice to the excitement that was coursing through her. Emilia Clark had always been her celebrity crush since she was sixteen and seeing her end up with the only basketball player she could claim she liked was the best news she could ever hear.

"It's been a long time coming," Meeka answered disinterested. She looked at her roommate, her fingers dancing on the screen as she swiped from one article to the other, jumping from one blog to another. "You know, there's a party the boys are organizing tonight. I've been invited, and you can come along also –"

"Don't do this now Meeka – not now please."

"What do you mean Laura?! Moreover, I think Tyrone is gonna be there. I don't see any reason why he wouldn't want to come out with his boys to celebrate the big moment. You could get a chance to meet him – I mean, I can push for someone to introduce us. I work there now." Meeka stood on her feet as she was certain she had convinced Laura.

"Okay. I'll go there – but just because I want to meet Tyrone. If we stay there and he does not show up, I'm outta there. Do you get that?"

"Oh chill out girl. You're going to a party and because – just because maybe Tyrone doesn't show up, you're gonna ignore all the fun. You need to get your head checked real soon

Laura." Meeka laughed at her and walked away into her bedroom.

2

"I don't think this is a good idea Meeka. Who do we know there?!" Laura fidgeted as they remained in the back seat of their taxi.

"Just fucking calm down Laura. It's a big boat party. You don't need to know anyone there. We just want to have some fun, so loosen up bitch."

"Well, it's easy for you to say that," she replied with a distant look on her face.

"What the fuck does that mean?" Meeka retorted.

"You know these guys don't play around – they just want to fuck you and be done. No strings attached."

"And you think you don't need a good drilling yet? You're rusting girl, and someone needs to grease your honeypot before it begins to shed its beauty." Meeka pushed the door to the taxi open and got out. "Just come on, let's enjoy the party and have fun for one night."

The boat was docked next to a large expanse of field and the dropping cadence of the sunny-ambient light reflecting against the water and back to the glossy white paint of the boat looked like what could pass for the best artwork of any artist. There were few people on the field, talking, mostly about business and even at that, they all looked calm and free. Jonathan Young was standing at the entrance of the boat, his phone to his ear. He raised his hand to Meeka when he saw her and waved her to come along.

"Mr. – sorry, Jonathan," she corrected herself immediately.

"I'll talk to you later Barbara; I've got to go." He ended the phone conversation without waiting for a response from the caller at the other end. "You'll get used to it in no time Meeka," he said and smiled at her while playing his eyes at Laura.

"This is my roommate, Laura. Laura this is Jonathan, he's one of my bosses at work," Meeka did the quick introduction. "I'm sorry, but I had to drag her out here. She would have preferred to sit at home and listen to her loser songs."

"Don't worry. I'm sure she will be glad you brought her here by tomorrow morning."

"She is here only because I told her that Tyrone would be here. Is there any chance he decided to hang out with the boys tonight?" Meeka inquired.

Jonathan's lips parted, revealing his white set of teeth. "You're just in luck because he arrived a few minutes ago, but he won't be staying long. I will introduce you to him." Jonathan led them onto the boat where the party was in full swing. The hip-hop music was blasting, and it was almost impossible to hear what someone next to you was saying – unless you stood next to them, nose almost touching each other. The crowd was not a big one, but it was plenty enough to fill every corner of the boat. After rubbing bodies with sweaty dancers, drunk hookers and heavenly-high athletes, we finally broke through to get to Tyrone Dub. He was having a conversation with Seam Nile and

Big Joe. They were laughing when Jonathan broke in.

"Hey man!" Jonathan shouted as they shook hands and patted each other's back. "So you're off the market huh? We're really gonna miss your plays man," he added.

"I'm still gonna getto hang out wid ma guys – that's for sure," Tyrone said in his diluted southern accent.

"That's great man," he replied and turned to face Meeka and Laura. "I don't think you've met our new intern, Meeka. She just started work today, and she brought her friend Laura. They came out here to have a good time with the guys."

The three guys welcomed the girls and Jonathan slipped away to let them "have a good time with the guys."

"I've always loved you since the first time you joined the Jaguars from Cali Phoenix," Laura said to Tyrone, her face fully flushed.

"I wanted a change of environment, and it's been really good to be here. In fact, it got really better tonight."

"Yeah. I love your wife too. Ever since I was a teen, I have always loved her characters. She does it for me just like you do it for me and I'm just glad the both of you found each other."

"Wouldn't you love to meet her? I can arrange for you to see her you know!"

"That would be so great!" Laura yelped.

"Let me have your digits, and I can call you to arrange things with you." Tyrone gave her his phone, and she typed her number in. "Laura right?" he asked as he added her name and pressed the save button. "You enjoy the party.

I'm just gonna say hi to a few more people and be outta here." He walked away from her and soon he was already occupied with another discussion.

Big Joe and Seam Nile were already hooked on Meeka's charm, and she was drooling all over them, so Laura walked to get herself a drink. She was sipping at her Long Island Iced Tea when Jonathan joined her at the bar. "That's the life, Laura. Everyone here understands that" Jonathan whispered to her.

"What life is that?" Laura inquired and took another sip of her drink.

"You know, there's a lot of demand on the players, and they need to be able to chill out. They need to have something that does not make them feel like they need always to be committed. That's where the girls come in. They know what they want too. No one here is looking for stability, just a fun night and we all move on to the next fun night to come along."

"Okay. So why are you telling me this?"

"I can see the way you're looking at Meeka. It's the kind of look a mother will give her daughter when she's not satisfied with her actions but can do nothing about it."

"It just doesn't make sense. When there are people who are ready to commit to you, I wonder why anyone will pick this over that."

"This is not a bad thing Laura. This is not what we do every day. Most of us have a life outside of this. We have partners, but there will always be a time that you need to purge yourself of all that commitment so that it doesn't kill you. The goal is always to remain healthy."

"I can see you've formed your opinion on the issue," Laura said and drained her glass.

"Not just an opinion. I've been on both sides, and I know what I'm talking about. I doubt you've ever had to do this before?"

"Nah. I'm not that kinda person," she answered.

"How do you know that if you've never tried it before?" Jonathan looked at the bartender. "Fill our glasses," he said and turned back to Laura. "Not everyone here wanted or thought they could be doing this. And it's not like it's a really bad idea."

"So what are you trying to do now?" Laura asked as she drank.

"You're a pretty girl Laura, and it looks like it's been a while since you had it good. I have the keys to some private room. We can go hang out alone together in there."

"Oh. I see. Is that why you're trying to get me drunk?"

"I don't need to do that. You're a big girl, so I expect you to be able to control yourself. If you don't want to drink, you don't have to. It's just that I drink a lot and my cool remains intact even after."

Laura smiled and looked at the older man. "You're good. I like you," she said and downed the rest of her drink. "Let's go." She stood up and looked at where she had seen Meeka last, and she was gone, as well as Big Joe and Seam Nile.

****

"Dig it in – push in harder!" Meeka cried as Big Joe stood on top of her, rushing into her like a waterfall from a mountain. "Don't stop fucking me, Big Joe. I want you to fuck me harder. Fuck me harder Big Joe!"

"Oh bitch! Shut the hell up!" Big Joe yelled at her as he rested his abs on her and rushed in faster. Few seconds later, his legs were twitching and his eyes flickering as he pumped his seed into her. Meeka pushed him off her back.

"You crazy or what? Your pull-out game is zero man. You ready to be a daddy?" she yelled at him and rushed into the bathroom. She turned the water on and tried to flush some of his cum out of her vagina. When she was done, she walked back to the room, picked a container from her bag and popped two pills into her mouth. "You should teach your friend never to do that again!" she said to Seam Nile before walking out of the room.

She went back to the party, searching for Laura so they could leave but she couldn't find her. She had gone around the boat and was about to go out to see if she had gone out to sit on the field when she noticed him. He was just arriving at the party, standing close to the steps, his hands in the pocket of his red Gucci joggers. His intimidating height of six foot seven, well-muscled body and the mouth-watering handsomeness of his face made him the sexiest player in the league. He knew this, and he flaunted it well with the glossy, well-trimmed low cut on his head, the Gucci labeled t-shirt he wore, the Yeezy boots and Rolex wristwatch. He looked around, saw one of his teammates and gave a heart-melting smile. He had the perfect set of teeth she had ever seen. Even from afar off, she could see his clipped nails as they glinted. She couldn't stop herself from wetting her pants again.

"Bobby fucking Bannon. You're never on time my nigga!" Teddy Moore yelled as he welcomed the man with a hug. "The party ain't over yet so come join in the groove." Teddy began to drag him away, and that was the first time she noticed that there was a girl standing next to him. She was the gorgeous type. She had everything. Her eyes were the color of fresh hazelnuts, thick glossy dark hair, long neck that had the curve of a flying saucer at the base. Her boobs were not too large to be held comfortably in a man's hand, and she had just the right size of ass. As Meeka stood there, she could imagine what her vagina would look like. She could see it lined with lilies and decorated with brightly shinning lapis lazuli.

 "Let's get out of here –" Laura's voice brought her back to reality, and she saw Bobby Bannon and his mistress disappear into the party.

 "Yeah. Let's get out of here," she agreed, and they walked off the boat.

3

Meeka was stirring her coffee after adding milk and sugar. She took a sip and dropped it back on the kitchen counter so she could serve herself more scrambled egg. Laura walked into the living room just then; her eyes were still heavy with sleep.

"So you decided to get up uh?" Meeka taunted her as she carried her tray to the living room.

"I just came to get my purse bitch. I left it here last night," Laura replied and swept the red purse off the chair.

"Are you going to tell me where you were last night while I was looking for you?"

"Where else do you think? I was fucking your boss dummy!" Laura replied and began walking back to the bedroom.

"Which boss?"

"Oh fuck! Which other boss did you introduce me to? I'm talking about Jonathan."

"You fucked Jonathan? And you were acting morally superior yesterday. You didn't even want to hear about the party yet you fucked my boss – bravo girl. I think I can begin to try liking you now."

Laura giggled. "Oh! Shut the hell up Meeka. I bet you did both guys yesterday – the look on your face when we left was unmistakable."

"No. The face was totally about something else. Those two guys fucked up. The burly one came inside me and didn't even apologize. But then I saw this other guy. I've heard a lot about him and seen pictures but seeing him in person; I lost my breath for a moment where I stood."

"Some of those players are just pure assholes," Laura agreed and began to smile mischievously. "The other guy, who is he?" She blinked her eyes at Meeka as her coy smile soon grew into a raucous laughter.

"Bobby Bannon – but I can't talk about him right now. I've got to be at work in fifteen," she said and drained the rest of her coffee down her throat.

"You can't avoid sharing that gist babe," Laura yelled out at her.

"I am not trying to," Meeka replied. She picked up her bag from the chair and walked out of the house as the clock struck seven-forty two. She walked into the office; Old Johnny was already sweating from his armpit. He gestured for her to come as soon as he sighted her. She remembered that he wasn't in the party from the previous night.

"Morning boss!" she smiled at him.

"We can exchange pleasantries later. Right now, I need you to run through these ledgers and find me something I haven't seen in it. I don't like losing even the tiniest dime on any money I control. Get it done right away."

"Yes sir!" Meeka drooled and walked to her cubicle. She remained there for the rest of the morning, and even when Jonathan came to talk to her, she had to excuse herself. It was not until lunch break before she had a few minutes of free time to herself. She had gone out to get herself a burger meal and also got Old Johnny a box of pizza on the way back.

"If it's not the busiest lady in the whole organization – I see you're finally free," Jonathan piped as he walked towards her cubicle.

"I thought every day would be like yesterday," Meeka belched silently as she replied. "Now I understand why there are always long queues in the coffee room. Once you sit in your chair, you might as well kiss every other activity goodbye till you are done."

"That's one of the reasons we're productive Meeka. We don't joke around, but it doesn't mean we don't joke cos we do a lot of that too."

"I can get used to this. It's not the worst way to work." Meeka paused before she continued. "Laura told me about last night," she chipped in.

Jonathan smiled calmly. "I bet she did – that one is a vixen beneath all the shades she's put on."

"I guess I have to say thank you for helping her have fun. She needed it badly," Meeka said.

"What about you?" Jonathan walked into her cubicle and let his keister rest on her table. He stretched his long legs forward and placed his hands on the desk.

"What about me?" Meeka inquired as she stared quizzically at the coy smile forming on his face.

"Did you have a good time or did those boys not treat you right?" he replied.

"I don't think I wanna talk about that Jonathan. It was a great party, and I enjoyed my time there," Meeka replied.

"But not as much as you wished it would have been right? I saw the disappointment in your eyes when you were leaving with Laura."

"So you saw us leaving, but you didn't come see us off!" Meeka attacked him.

"I saw that you just wanted to leave and I didn't want to look overbearing, so I let you go," Jonathan answered.

"Whatever," Meeka grunted.

"And that's one thing I don't like. I fucking hate it when people don't say what they've got in their mind," he yelled and stood up from the desk.

"You either fucking man up and speak, or you come get a good fuck for the day," he blurted. "Ooopss!" he whispered and walked back to sit with the edge of his butt on the table.

"Okay," Meeka said. She shaded her face with no expression, staring into his eyes.

"What – wha – what do you mean by okay?" Jonathan stammered.

"Let's fuck," Meeka replied. "After work," she added.

"Oh!"

"Or were you just joking when you said that?"

"Nope. No chance in hell that I was just joking. I just didn't think you would go for that option, but it's all good though," he rushed and stood up from the table again. "I guess I'll be seeing you in a few hours Meeka," he said.

"You will," Meeka replied.

Jonathan walked closer to her and whispered into her ear. "Make sure you don't touch yourself thinking about what I will do to you," he said and walked away, a cocky smile playing on his face.

****

"I have processed all the account. I also came up with the report for the board," Meeka said as she dropped the file in her hand on Old Johnny's table. "I heard you are talking about it," she added when she saw the confused stare on his face.

"Okay. Thank you Meeka," Old Johnny replied. "– and you've waited way past your closing time. You can leave whenever you want to."

"I'm just getting my job done sir," Meeka answered before she walked out of the office. She went back to her workspace and began to pack her things. "I'm outta here Old Johnny," she said as she stood by his door. Old Johhny raised his eyes from the file he was looking through.

"Oh! Alright," he stammered as he still tried to focus on what he was looking at. "I'll see you tomorrow then."

"Yeah," Meeka answered and walked away. She walked down the row of offices that three of the seven directors use before turning into the corner where Jonathan's office sat. Naomi, his secretary, wasn't on seat anymore, so she went ahead to knock on his door. In few seconds he opened it.

"I thought you already had your fill in the toilet for the day," Jonathan said as he walked back to take his seat.

Meeka closed the door behind her. "I prefer to have the real deal most times," she answered and gave him a mischievous smile.

"How do you want to go about this? We could head over to any hotel or –"

"Here's just fine" Meeka interrupted. She got up and inched her skirt up. "Come on and let's get going," she urged him before pulling her panties down. Jonathan jumped to his feet. He fumbled with his belt as he walked round to her side.

His eyes widened when he got to her, and he looked down. "I fucking the love the bulge on your clit," Jonathan exclaimed.

"Just shut the fuck up and dig in," Meeka sighed. Her hand found its way past his trouser, and she began to rub him hard. The texture of his short boxer was light, and in seconds he was solid as a rock. "Now, get to it," she said and inched forward on his table. Jonathan took her from behind. He slipped in with ease, and she shuddered only a little from his entry.

"You've had lots," he commented, but she said nothing. He coursed in and out of her, taking his time to direct every movement he made. He was making a mental calculation of his rigid length and width, his entry length and angle – how he could twist himself around inside her to hit all the touchy spot at every return journey but his first few thrusts didn't steal a sound from her. He was making his sixth push when the first noise escaped her mouth. It was a silent one, but he knew he was beginning to do it right, so he kept pushing into her. Few more of shoving his long head into her, he had her all screaming and pipping. She couldn't keep quiet anymore, and he had to cover her mouth with one of his hand while the other fumbled with her breast so their noise wouldn't ring through the whole building. "Do you like how I'm fucking you?" he mumbled as he kept his pace steady.

"Just fuck me – don't talk," Meeka replied and bit his hand in her mouth gently. "Go harder!" she added and bit harder on his finger.

"Fuck you!" Jonathan yelled as he felt the pain course through his finger down to his feet. He let his feet press on the ground to keep him steadier as he pushed into her with more energy. Her sweet moaning had now turned into a soft cry for help as she felt the numbing sensation starting to build up inside her. Meeka's feet began to wobble, as the throbbing traveling through her grew heavier with each thrust Jonathan completed. When she couldn't take it any longer, she pushed him off her back and turned to face him. She got out of her clothes in a flash of lightning.

"Don't fucking slow down now," she mumbled with the mist of ecstasy still swirling around her. She pulled him back in between her wide-spread thighs and pressed her lips against his. She held his buttocks with her hands and pushed him into her. She went stiff for almost three seconds, her heart stopped, and she could feel her blood slowly moving through her veins. "Fuck this!" she exclaimed when she finally came to and continued helping him push his buttocks into her. Her moans were beginning to grow wild, and even Jonathan could not concentrate on keeping her quiet as he could feel himself getting close to the peak. "Yeah – yeah – yeah. I like the way you fuck me, Jonathan, ravish me – my entire being baby," she stammered.

"I'm gonna cum," Jonathan whispered. "Bring it on me," Meeka answered.

"Here we go," Jonathan removed himself from inside her and Meeka dropped flat on the table. Jonathan let his penis rest on her navel as his seed rushed out and poured on her. At the same time, he had his hands working on her clit as she began to shudder. Meeka had to bite on her finger to keep herself from shouting the whole building down as the last, and perfect travel of pure pleasure and blissful ecstasy came down on her. She remained on the table for almost a minute, trying to recover from the quick five minutes of a memorable sex.

"You fuck really good sir," she said when she made it to sit on the chair still naked.

"And you know how to make the right sounds," Jonathan replied. He pulled his trousers and boxers back up before taking his seat. "You definitely can make a man stuck on you. You've really got something to give Meeka," he eyed her and laughed.

Meeka tore from a tissue paper on his table and cleaned his cum off her belly. "This is one fuck I will remember; I can promise you that Jonathan," she replied. She picked up her clothes from the floor and began to done them. "You know what Big fucking Joe did yesterday? The nigga came inside me without thinking twice! Can you imagine that shit!" she yelled as she adjusted her skirt.

"Well, that's something. I knew that Big Joe was beginning to slack in the game, I just never thought that he would dwindle in this action too," Jonathan commented.

"He's fucked up," Meeka added. "I've got to go now. I closed later than usual and then spent more time here," she said as she picked her bag up.

"Alright Meeka. I will see you tomorrow then," Jonathan said and gave her another smile. Meeka half-smiled and walked out of the door. She walked out of the corner that Jonathan's office was sitting back to the hallway and headed for the elevator. She had pressed the button and was waiting when Bobby Bannon walked up to her side. She had not noticed him walking out of one of the offices behind her when she walked out from Jonathan's corner.

"Hey," Bobby greeted her.

Meeka's eyes shone brightly as she looked up and saw him. "Hey Bobby," she answered. "I didn't see you come up behind me," she added.

"It looked like you were focused on leaving here," Bobby replied.

"Not that. I closed late, and I just want to get home."

"I know how that feels my dear," he commented.

"I'm sure you do. When the season starts again, I wonder how you manage to remain sane with all the training."

"It's my job. I've got to remain sane to win the game babe."

"I'm Michelle, others call me Meeka, but you can call me Michelle," Meeka said and smiled, baring her teeth at him.

"Well Michelle, it's great meeting you," Bobby answered, and the elevator door slid open. They walked into the elevator car.

"So I've watched all of your games for the last three years, and man, you have been great!"

"That's the goal Michelle, but we don't just play to be great, we play great so that our fans can feel great too," he replied smoothly. He had the habit of licking his lips as he spoke and Meeka could not help herself from finding it hot and sexy.

"I love how you play so much," she added, and Bobby only smiled. Michelle looked and saw that they were on the fifth floor already. She couldn't wait for long – she had to act immediately. She turned to Bobby. "Can I get an autograph?" she requested.

"Definitely. Where would you like to have it?"

Meeka pulled off her t-shirt and pulled up her brassiere. "I hope this is okay?" she asked and smiled at him again.

"Sure," Bobby replied. He removed a pen from his pocket and penned his initials on her breast crossing over her nipples, and she let out a slight yelp. "I'm sorry about that," he apologized and dropped the pen back in his pocket.

Meeka smiled at him and covered herself up. "It's okay," she said. "Anything for Bonny Bannon."

"Well, you've got really great boobs. I won't mind having them some time," Bobby said and smiled coyly at her.

"I'm sure that could be arranged as soon as you want it," Meeka replied.

"We'll see about that." The elevator door opened and they walked out. "Michelle, it was really nice meeting you."

"You bet it was," Michelle replied and walked away as Bobby headed for his car.

4

It had been three long days since Michelle spoke with Bobby and exposed her boobs for him in the elevator. She had gone to work every day, working during office hours then fucking Jonathan afterward before going home. Every single one of those days, she had always hoped she would run into Bobby, but that was yet to happen. While she waited for the day she would meet him again, she had met other players, and it had progressed quickly with them. She had followed Yari Tate and Ian McKinley home after work one day. She spent the night in their apartment, and then hurried home to get prepared before rushing back to the office. She had to apologize to Jonathan for not showing up for their usual fuck event the previous evening. To make things right between them, she had shown up early to work the next day, extremely early and she fucked him before everyone else arrived – even her boss, Old Johnny. Luckily for her, which had not really happened since she started working, she was able to get herself free for lunch, so she decided to treat herself. She went to the new restaurant that was just across their building. She was savoring the taste of her burger when her phone buzzed – it was an unknown caller ID, but she picked it nonetheless.

"Yeah, hello…" she said. Her face lit up when she heard the person on the other end identify himself. "Hey Bobby. I've been wondering when you were going to give me a call," she divulged before she could keep herself from saying it. She listened to him talk with her face glowing with a radiant smile. "I would definitely love that," she answered, but her face carried a shade of gloom. "I'll see you there," she said and dropped the phone. She was almost leaping out of her seat when she dropped the phone if she had not looked around and remembered that she was in a restaurant, but she still managed to draw attention to herself with her raucous laughter. She paid her bills without finishing her lunch and ran back to the office. Most of the other workers were still out for lunch, so the office was deserted. She walked to Old Johnny's office, but he wasn't on sit, so she had to leave a message for him with his secretary.

"Agnes, please when Old Johnny comes back can you please tell him that my roommate was in an accident and she is badly hurt. I have to go check up on her," Meeka informed the woman before sprinting out of the office, her bag and belongings flying after her. She hailed down a cab and was soon en-route North Cove where she knew Bobby was patiently waiting for her. The boat looked deserted from afar, which was just what she wanted. She paid the cab driver and got down. She was still dressed in her office clothes, a green elbow length white cotton shirt with a neat bow dropping on the button on a blue satin skirt and matching shoes. She adjusted her skirt again before walking to the boat.

Meeka's opened mouth, wide with her biggest smile shut the moment she got onto the boat and saw the crowd. They were not much, she counted about twelve guys and less than half of that amount of girls – but it was still a crowd compared to what she had expecting. Bobby was laughing loudly to one of the girls that just jumped into the pool of alcohol they had made when he turned around and saw her standing apart. He excused himself from the rest and came to her.

"Hey, you made it – and fast too," he said and smiled at her. He kissed her cheek.

"Yeah. I didn't know it was a big party," Meeka replied.

"I'm sorry about that. It was supposed to be just me and you but then I called Levi, and he said he had to join in. He just finalized the divorce with his wife, and I just couldn't refuse him. Now I know I should have 'cause I had no idea he was coming with his own guests."

"It's okay. I guess the more, the merrier right!" Meeka said.

"Yeah, it is but you've got me for today though. Just me and you while the rest of them do whatever they want," Bobby answered.

Meeka gave him a half-smile. "Well, I can work with that," she said.

"That's great," Bobby said. "Come on let me introduce you to everyone." He walked her to the rest of the crowd. "Hey guys, this is Michelle," he said.

"But y'all can just call me Meeka. I'd prefer that in fact," she chipped in.

Bobby gave her a side look and smiled faintly. "Well, she's an intern with the accounting department of the team, so we're all gonna be seeing a lot of her I'm sure – or at least I can speak for myself," he said and blinked his eyes at her. Everyone said hello before going back to their game. "And that's it, let's just head inside so we can have some privacy," Bobby added and led her beneath the boat.

"Why'd you decide to have your internship with Jaguars? There are other amazing financial institutions out there that you could have learned even better," Bobby asked as they took their seat on the cushion in the lower deck.

"I've always loved basketball. I've always loved Jaguars. I've always loved watching you play. Why would I give up the opportunity of getting close to all these things and to a special someone?"

"That answers it well," Bobby said and laughed lightly. He stood up and walked towards the bar that was still looking neat which meant none of those ups have been down yet. "Do you want me to fix you a drink? I used to be a bartender for a while back in Texas, and I was pretty damn good at it too."

"Definitely," Meeka answered. "I'm certain I'd take poison if you prepared it for me," she said and laughed it off as a joke, but the confused look that remained on Bobby's face afterward made her realize he didn't take it as a joke.

"You really shouldn't do that though Michelle, the guy's just gonna go ahead and get a new bitch to dig into whenever he feels the need," Bobby said. "But hey, you really do turn me on when you talk like that," he added. He pressed his head forward, drinks still in his hand and kissed her. He handed her a glass of Cognac and sat down next to her.

"I really like you, Bobby," she confessed.

"I do like you too Michelle. I mean that's why you're here or don't you think so?"

"I saw you with the other girl back at that party you guys threw some days ago. Are you serious about her or it's just a fling?"

"I see you're already trying to mark your territory– I like that Michelle," Bobby said. "Well, Michelle and I have an understanding, and that includes that I can see whoever I want or get serious with whoever I want."

"I think I like the sound of that. You know, coming from a player like you."

"What do you mean by a player like me? What type am I? In fact what kinda player are you talking about?" Bobby asked with a shade of smile on his face, so she does not think he was rattled by her question.

"Well, you know –" Meeka began, "you've got a lot of girls who throw themselves at you at every corner, but you can still decide that you wanna get serious with someone. I like that – and I was only talking about you as a basketball player," she added.

"And you don't mind that I am a player in the other sense?"

"You're not a player Bobby. Or at least, that's the way I see it," Meeka replied. "You're a young talented, good looking and rich star, who wouldn't want you? Everyone knows you will always have a flock of girls around you so whoever expects that you should be stuck to anyone doesn't know what they're doing – it's not like you're hiding the other girls you bang from them."

"You've just made it to the top of my list Michelle. You're my number one girl from now on," Bobby said and laughed. "You really understand how these things work with us," he said.

"I'm just that kind of girl," Meeka replied and smiled to herself as she took a sip of her drink. "We can get to it whenever you are ready; I'm always ready to –" she couldn't finish her sentence before Bobby covered her mouth with his.

"That felt good," Meeka commented when he pulled away. She inched closer to him and replaced her lips on his. She sucked him till she was filled with too much of him, but even then she still wouldn't break away. Ready to choke on Bobby's breathe, Meeka finally broke the kiss when the door to the lower deck opened and she heard the voice of other people.

"Oh sorry, guys. We had no idea something interesting was going on in here," one of them mumbled and laughed.

"Yeah, if we had, you should know that I would have made sure we knocked before coming in," another said and this time all of them burst into laughter.

"Guys, cut it!" Bobby yelled out, and they all went quiet. "You can all leave now. You can see that it is a private party in here right?"

"Oh Bobby. Come on, you really don't wanna do that, and you know it," the first guy said again.

"Derrick, not today – maybe another time," Bobby commented.

"Bobby, you know how it feels at the end, don't you. Let's do this – it's been a long time coming. I know Meeka here won't mind," the third guy said.

"Tom, you shouldn't be the one doing this to me – you know that," Bobby said, his tone already placid now. He turned to Meeka who had been quiet all the while, confused with what the men were talking about.

"What? What are you guys talking about?" she inquired. She looked at the four men standing by the door, waiting for a response to what she couldn't figure out yet.

"I don't really know how to go about asking you this Michelle, but I'm just going to say it, so it doesn't sound so derogatory," Bobby started. "The guys and I, we have something we usually do – it's more like something we do for fun rather than using to show power. It helps us cool down after all the heat with the game you know."

"Just fucking say what it is Bobby and stop scaring me," Meeka replied.

"Okay. We are kinda like into bukakee – you know, that Japanese kinda gangbang," he said.

Meeka looked at him weirdly. "Are you fucking serious about this?"

"I knew you wouldn't be cool with it. Just forget that I asked. Can you please do that?" Bobby pleaded and stood up on his feet.

"What the fuck is this nigga talking 'bout. I'd love to get into that shit right now," she yelled and smiled at the guys who were already smiling ear to ear. Meeka stood up and moved closer to Bobby. "But you'll owe me a good one on one fuck after we're done here," she whispered into his ear.

"You bet. I won't forget that," Bobby answered and kissed her. "Let's get to it niggas," he said to the guys, and they all walked closer. Meeka went back to sit on the cushion while she let the guys take her clothes off her body. She watched them take their time, loosening every button, pulling at every zip, tugging at her clothes, their hands crawling on her skin, their fingers grazing her nipples that were still covered by her brassiere. Meeka pushed all five men off her as she unhooked her bra, dropped it on the cushion and peeled her panties off her hips. They got out of their clothes too, their longs standing stiff, ready to go.

"Let's get this party started!" Tom yelled out, and they all came at her as though she were the first human they were seeing in their zombie-land after decades of no visitors. She watched Bobby go for the pot of honey between her legs, and she smiled to herself. Derrick climbed onto the cushion. He held his dick in his hands, pried her mouth open and let himself in.

"You suck this well Meeka. Let me feel your tongue curling on the big guy here," he laughed and began to push in and out of her mouth. Meeka could feel the whole width of Tom inside her mouth, hitting all the walls of her gum and even going as deep, almost into her throat. She looked up at him, a pretty smile on his face, his hands at the base of his penis, giving himself the support he needed. At the same time, Tom had her hands on his, giving him a sweet massage on his erect head. Bobby was down on her, slowly licking away at her pussy before Doug came. He headed straight for her and while the others were still busy, he tapped her to turn over. Only three people were going to have access to her with her current position. Derrick cursed as

Meeka dragged his dick out of her mouth and she turned on her back, her head resting out of the chair. Derrick went down from the chair and ran to her front so he could continue. Meeka looked towards Bobby and signaled for him to get under her on the cushion. Martin finally took his position behind her, and he wasted no time going in through her ass. The last man in the group was Jim, but he stood on one side, fondling with her breast as he jerked off with the other. Bobby slid under her onto the cushion so she could finally let her hips down. As she dropped down, she fell onto Bobby's hard rock penis, and that was the first time she felt someone that deep inside her. Within minutes, most of the holes on her body were filled up and feeling heavy, her mouth, her ass, and her tight pussy were beginning to feel like they were not existing and it remained that way till the men changed position. Thirty minutes later when they were finishing up, Meeka could almost not feel anything apart from the high level of excitement and the raging pleasure that was running through her.

"Come kneel here Meeka," Martin commanded and pointed at the space where they had left for her in the middle. Meeka walked in and fell on her knees. The men were all gently rubbing away at their dicks as they were just a few seconds away from pouring it all out. They inched closer to Meeka as they felt the rush coming through the narrow pipe that led to the tip of the hole and when it finally came, it looked like a rainstorm in the middle of summer. Meeka's head had soon become a web of milky strands, and her face looked like buttered bread with a sparse layer of thin mayonnaise.

"This one is a good one," Tom commented as he exhaled and sat down on the cushion.

"Yeah, I agree with that," Jim added. "You keep her close Bobby."

Meeka crawled to the cushion and sandwiched herself in between Tom and Jim till she regained enough strength to walk to the bathroom to wash herself. Bobby remained on the floor exhaling hard as the other men dressed up and left the room for him and Meeka.

"Did you like that?" Bobby asked. He pushed himself off the floor.

"To be honest, for my first time trying it out, it was really great, and I won't mind trying it again," she answered.

"I'm glad you liked it. But you should know that next time; we only do it if you want it too."

Meeka looked back at him from the bathtub where she was washing the cum off her body. "Awwnn! You're so considerate." She walked out of the tub, dripping and kissed him. "I've got to go though. I have to catch up on some work at home before I resume work tomorrow," she said.

"Okay. That's good," Bobby murmured. "I'm going to call you later. We should hang out more – just you and me."

"I've told you, Bobby, anything for Bobby Bannon," she replied. She kissed him one more time before walking away.

5

"Please repeat what you just said," Laura was yelling at the top of her voice.

"I said I fucking had sex with Bobby," Meeka answered.

"And how did this happen? I want fucking details Meeka. Give me the full gist," Laura pressed.

"Leave the details out of the question Laura – like you gave me the details of the night out with Jonathan. You just told me you two were together and that was all," she shrugged.

"You're such a whore Meeka. How did you get him to fuck you?"

"We met in the elevator after work about three days ago, and we got talking. I guess he took a liking to me, so he called me during lunch and invited me on his boat," Meeka answered.

"He has a boat too – you picked the right one Meeka. So just the two of you on that big boat? I bet you guys did it everywhere on the boat." Laura chuckled as she jumped up and down on her seat waiting for Meeka to divulge more information.

"Okay, I'm going to tell you, but you have to promise to keep your mouth shut. You cannot tell anyone about this," Meeka said.

Laura immediately crossed her hands over her chest. "I cross my heart Meeka. Tell me now!"

"It wasn't just Bobby; he had other friends with him. One of them just finalized his divorce, so he brought guys and some ladies to come party on the boat," Meeka started. "Bobby and I went to the lower deck, and we were making out about to go to third base when some of the other guys came in. They joined in, and we all had a good time."

"No fucking way you're going to say that and not give more details. I want to hear everything that happened after those other guys came in. You were in a fucking gangbang right?" The excitement in her voice was reverberating.

"You're such an asshole, Laura. You know if it were you, you wouldn't be telling me all these – you would just walk straight to your room and keep mute like it didn't happen."

"I think that's why we're different. Or don't you think so?"

"Whatever," Meeka said and readjusted herself in the seat before she continued with her story. "The guys came in; they pressed Bobby till he agreed to let them all fuck me. It looked like they were used to doing that kinda stuff together and I wanted to see what it would feel like so I agreed to it – and that's all the story so let me be now."

"You're a whore – totally. You can even decide to do it for a living because you're so good at it. Aren't you?"

"Just shut the fuck up and make dinner. I'm famished right now. I didn't finish my lunch, and I didn't have anything at Bobby's."

"You're the one who wanted dicking, and you got it – even more than you hoped for. I don't know why that didn't fill you up."

"Fuck you, Laura," Meeka yelled, then jumped to her feet. "I'll just get something to keep me from devouring you before you're done with dinner." She walked to the refrigerator, pulled out a packet of potato chips and poured herself a glass of milk.

"But you gotta be careful with these people Meeka. They only gonna look out for themselves – or themselves first."

"It's just sex Laura – nothing else. Or what were you thinking I wanted?"

"Well, I know the girl Bobby's currently dating, Imani. We grew up on the same street in Queens, and she was a total nutcase. I don't think she's really done with her old life and even if she is, I'm sure she can still reach out to people who can help her take care of the trouble."

"So what are you saying? That I am trouble?"

"No. Definitely not. I just don't want to see you get hurt Meeka," Laura countered.

"I can take care of myself, Laura. Moreover, Bobby said he's cutting her away a little bit. I'm his go-to girl for now, so I don't have to worry about shit. I'm not fighting for her man – I already have her man."

"Okay. If that's what you're saying." She stood up and walked to the kitchen. "I'm now going to cook so you can eat. You need your energy for when Bobby's gonna call you to come fuck again." She dabbed her lashes at her and tumbled over with laughter.

"Just do your fucking job Laura and stay out of my business," Meeka chuckled as she walked back to the chair to devour her chips and milk.

****

"Meeka, where the fuck were you yesterday? I fucking called your number, and it just wouldn't go through!" Old Johnny was yelling silently as he stood by her desk. She could feel his anger suffusing.

"I told Agnes why I had to leave early sir. My friend was in an accident, and I had to go make sure she was fine," Meeka replied. "You could ask her –"

"Just shut the fuck up. I asked her, and she told me, I just wanted to see how you would react when you go to see the boss at the top," he said and laughed.

"I'm sorry, what did you say?"

"You're going to see the boss – didn't you hear me clearly the first time?"

"I wasn't sure it was me you were talking to me – and you know it would be really disastrous to assume."

"Whatever, just make sure you are prepared to go see him. I will come get you when I'm ready," Old Johnny said and began to walk away.

"We're going together?" Meeka inquired, her brows ruffled.

"Of course! Did you think I was gonna send you in there on your own? Just that the man could decide to ignore me and talk to you, so I need you to be in your best game – no fuckups. You get that?"

"To the last dot sir," she replied. Meeka watched her boss walk away. He smiled at some of the others at adjoining cubicle and then he would suddenly frown at another. She shook her head and took her seat. She had been staring at numbers on her computer screen for hours, yet waiting to hear Old Johnny shout her name from the front of his office so they could go see the boss together, but when she felt the tap on her shoulders, she thought he had decided to do things differently.

"I'm just going to be a moment sir," she said as she ruffled through the papers she had gathered for the meeting only to turn around and be staring into Jonathan's eyes.

"Oh! Jonathan. It's you," she mumbled.

"Yeah, it's me," Jonathan replied. "You stood me up yesterday – again," he said.

"What do you mean?" Meeka queried.

"What do you mean what do I mean? We were supposed to meet yesterday after work as usual – you didn't show up again," he replied.

"Oh! That," Meeka exhaled. "I didn't know it was supposed to be an everyday ritual. I just thought we would go at it for a while, take a break, come back to it, take a break – not an everyday stuff you know," she said.

"Come on Meeka. You've given me a taste, and now you want to starve me so I will crave it more – I get what you're doing Meeka."

"Jonathan, I'm not doing anything. I just can't be fucking you every day. Where's the fun in that?" she shrugged and turned back to her computer.

"If that's how you want to play it then it's all good. We had a nice time together – if you're ever feeling horny while you're at work you know where to find me," Jonathan said and walked away.

"Well, that's a wrap," Meeka exhaled again and wiped off the sweat that wasn't on her face.

"Meeka! Get your ass over here now!" Meeka smiled when she heard the usual yell. "I'm right by your side Old Johnny!" she yelled back, picked up the file and ran to his office.

6

Meeka stood at the feet of the staircase that led to the boat, she wanted to cry, but she knew it was useless. Her tears would not help, and no one was going to take her seriously if they ever found her with tears on her face. She looked back up at the boat and saw Bobby looking down at her. She stared at him pleadingly, but he removed his face and walked away from sight. Meeka sighed and shook her head. All she wanted was to get what every other girl that was in her shoes wanted – just a small bit of the big chunk. She hailed down a cab and left for her apartment.

"I told you to watch out for yourself remember?" Laura cried when Meeka narrated her ordeal to her.

"And that was what I was trying to do – trust me," Meeka replied. She had been pacing around the living room since she got in.

"How do you call that watching out for yourself? You were literarily throwing yourself out there for him to do whatever he likes with you and he saw that," she argued.

"Do you think I am the only one he's got his eyes on Laura? Or do you think the other girls he messes around with are not thinking or even doing exactly what I am doing?"

"Just quit walking around the room for a minute. It's really disturbing," Laura yelled at her.

"Get used to it Laura. I'm trying to calm my nerves, and that's the only way I know how to do it."

"Fuck!" Laura cursed silently. "He doesn't want to see you again now so who do you think he's gonna go back to?"

"Either he sticks around Imani more these days, or he spends more time with his other side chicks," she answered.

"Which is exactly what you didn't want happening before. So you see that it wasn't a great idea to tie him down."

"A pregnancy isn't going to tie him down Laura. It's just going to get me the money I need to live in a comfortable condo – that's all I want. Or is that too much to ask for?"

"And you couldn't have told him that? Would he have refused to buy it for you?"

Meeka sighed. "You still don't get it Laura – you don't get it."

"Then explain it the fuck to me. At least I'm here to listen to you – not like you've been paying attention to any of my problems for the past three months."

"What the fuck does that mean Laura? You know I've always been here for you, ready to listen but you don't talk to me – or anybody that I know of."

"You mean like the night I came home after Jack dumped me and I cried my heart out on this very chair. I left you tens of messages, and you could not even reply me – or you want us to talk about when your boss also told me he wasn't interested anymore. Remember you were the one who asked me to give him a try. You weren't here then either, and I really wanted to talk to you, but you just weren't here," Laura replied and sighed.

"I didn't know all that Laura," Meeka replied with a calmer voice. "I really had no idea. I'm so sorry darling. Please, I'm so sorry," she pleaded like a puppy.

"I had gotten over that a long time ago. Just tell me what you were thinking – if you were thinking at all – when you decided not to use a condom," Laura replied.

"Let me explain this to you –" she started. "If I can have a baby for Bobby, he would have no choice but to pay child support till the baby becomes an adult which is in eighteen years. Do you think I would need to work one day before I get whatever I want if that happened? For eighteen years, I'll be able to get whatever I want, and before that time expires, I would have figured out how to make things better for the later years."

"So you just wanna trap him with a baby – that's all?"

"Yeah. What do you think? You think I wanna get married to that guy who cannot keep to a woman for just a night?" she chuckled. "That's never going to happen."

"And you wonder why he's pissed at you and doesn't want you anymore?"

"I'm just wondering why he's pissed at just me 'cause I know that's what the rest of the girls he's with are planning Laura. I'm not the only one –even Imani has the same goal."

"Well, that's fucked, I thought this was just fun for you – nothing serious---" Laura exhaled. "You're gonna have to move on with your life Meeka. That chapter is closed already so come back – maybe you can begin to think about getting a job with your degree."

"I don't want a job, Laura. That's too stressful for too little money," she replied.

"If you go back to Jaguars, I'm sure they'll be ready to give a more permanent job this time. Old Johnny would even put in a word for you I'm sure."

"I fucking abandoned my internship there Laura. I'm sure they don't wanna see me – especially Old Johnny."

"It's just been two weeks since you didn't show up there. I'm sure you can think of something to tell them, and they're gonna have you back in no time. Moreover, Jonathan has this thing for you, make good use of that," Laura pressed.

"Before the last two weeks, I was not focused a lot in the last one month. I'm sure they don't want me – not even giving Jonathan another good fucking will make him want to help me," she replied.

"Well, I can say I have tried as a friend," Laura exhaled as she stood up from the cushion and walked into her room.

"Fuck! Fuck! Fuck! Fuck me!" Meeka yelled out and kicked against the foot of the cushion. She jumped up and sat on the cushion holding her toe. "Fuck! Everything is just out to get me today." She remained on the chair as she thought on how she was going to go about her life.

*****

Meeka walked into the room in an exquisite black gown Bobby had bought for her when they went shopping together some weeks back. She was in a matching black Versace stiletto with the glowing head of Medusa brightening her feet.

She looked around the crowd that had graced the party, and she nodded – it was definitely where she wanted to be. When she Kelly, one of the girls she had become friends with while she was with Bobby told her of the fundraiser, she knew she had to be there. It was organized by Jaguars board for the players, and she knew all the team members would be there which meant she was getting a new guy for herself tonight. That was her assignment for the night.

She took confident strides and soon got lost in the crowd. She met a few people she had made acquaintance within the past few months she was with Bobby. She exchanged pleasantries before heading to the bar to take her position. She ordered her first shot of drink and sent it down her throat with a single throw. The next three went down simultaneously within a two minutes interval which was when she saw who she was going for.

Tommy Wiles had just walked into the hall with no woman in his arms which could only mean one thing – he intended to take someone from the party home. He had been part of the gangbang that happened on Bobby's boat. He was not amongst the top fifty guys she would fuck, but she was ready to just go with him till whenever her plan to get Bobby back fell in place. Tommy had also noticed her sitting at the bar all alone, and he walked toward her.

"And who do we have here," he smacked his lips at her.

"Hey Tommy," she half-smiled at him.

"I think fuck-break looks good on you Meeka. You are looking fucking take-home-to-bed," he said.

"Who said I was on a fuck-break?" Meeka countered.

"Well that's true, isn't it? It doesn't mean cos Bobby is out of the picture you can no longer get people to give you a good feel," he replied.

"It's just what it is Tom. Life goes on; the pussy needs to get greased regularly to keep it sweet and smooth for great guys like you," she said with a tinge of lust. Her eyes glinted of want for him for a second, and he smiled.

"So that's what it's gonna be tonight?"

"Come on Tom. Are you going to say you haven't thought of having me to yourself since that day on the boat? I'm sure you don't want my mouth to be the only hole you'll tell the tale of filling with your cock – by the way, you've got a really huge cock there. It looks pretty too," she smiled at him again.

"Now I see why Bobby was stuck on you for a very long time," Tom said and laughed.

"What's that?"

"You're really sweet with your mouth – both in words, smiles, and sucking. You know how to use those two lips well Meeka," he answered.

"I've got two other lips that you've never had a taste of too. Sure you don't wanna try that out?"

"I would love to Meeka so what do you say we hit up after the whole party is done? We team members have gotta go do our duty now," he said and nodded towards the podium where the manager was climbing.

"I'm sure those kids really appreciate every penny you guys give them. You have a good heart," she added before turning to get herself more drinks. She smiled to herself before dropping from the bar stool and walking to the main event area. She had spotted Bobby sitting close to the front with Imani. She searched around for where Tom was. His table was just three tables away from Bobby's, and there was still one empty seat left, so she walked over there.

"I hope you boys won't mind me joining you here," she said as she took her seat. Tom smiled at her while the rest of the guys mumbled their approval. "Thank you, gentlemen," she added and smiled again. The manager was talking about all the projects they had done with the money they gathered from the fundraiser in the past six years in some African countries. They had built schools, hospitals, and stadiums for the kids in those countries and they wanted to improve on that. The new project was to build three universities in three different countries within the next three years, but they needed a lot of cash to start. Donations were well on the way, and by the end of the night, they had gathered three hundred million dollars in cash and check, and an extra four hundred million in pledge commitments.

"You see why I said you have a good heart? Giving out your hard-earned money to kids you have never met. That's really sweet," Meeka said to Tommy when the donations were done, and everyone was having a good time.

"We have to give back to the society Meeka. We make a lot so it is the least we can do," Tommy replied. They were still discussing when she saw Old Johnny walking up to her after speaking with the manager. She stood still, waiting for him to get to, her, anticipating what he was going to say to her.

"Meeka, you're looking gorgeous tonight," he smiled and kissed her on the cheek.

Meeka flushed. "Thank you, Old Johnny," she answered.

"It looks like your self-recommended break is working out just well for you," he said and grinned even harder.

"I would think it is," she answered and smiled back. "But I was thinking of coming back to work though," she threw it in without thinking. She bit her lips as she knew this was not the right place to talk about that.

"I was expecting that you would have told me that when you either returned one of the hundreds of calls placed to you or when you came to the office to see me concerning the issue."

"I'm sorry Old Johnny. It just kinda slipped," she apologized. "I had plans to come see you tomorrow actually," she added.

"Well, is that so!" he blunted and nodded to himself. "The door is always open Meeka. You know you can come see me any time," he said and smiled at her.

"Thank you so much, Old Johnny. I appreciate your help," she responded. The man smiled at her and walked away. "That went well didn't it?" she turned to Tommy who had been quiet while she spoke with her former boss.

"I'm sure it's going to be alright Meeka," he answered. "Or do you think anyone can stay mad at you for long?"

Meeka was smiling at his compliment when Imani walked up to her. She had not seen her coming at her, and even when she stopped in front of her she had been expecting she would move along, but Imani remained. "Can I help you?"

"Yeah, bitch. You can definitely help me. All I need is for you to stay away from my man. You don't come to wherever he is – just stay the hell away from him. Do you get that?" she yelled at her while pressing her face close to hers.

"Imani, can you please leave my face and go be with your man," Meeka said, "– as you call him," she added and smiled coyly at the other lady. Bobby walked up to the group just then. He grabbed Imani by the arm.

"Satin, I told you not to cause a scene here. We're leaving right away," he ordered and dragged her out of the hall. Meeka just stood there, taking in all the eyes that were staring at her and the hot-assed Imani that was walking away.

"Do you want to get out of here?"

Meeka responded immediately. "I thought you would never ask." She followed him out of the hall too, and the party returned to its gentle cadence.

7

Meeka had called Tom fifteen minutes ago to ask if he was at home but she knew he wasn't. He told her that he was still at Bobby's, but he was about leaving. They had agreed that she should go to his house and wait if he doesn't get there before him. They had been together for just about two weeks, and in that time, all they had done was fuck – nothing else. So when she called him, he had assumed she was down for another fucking episode. Meeka's taxi parked out front by the roadside on the street. She waited for a moment in the taxi, going over everything once again ensuring her plan was airtight. When she had reassured herself it was going to work, she paid the taxi driver and came out. She looked at the familiar houses at both sides and heaved another sigh out of her lungs. She looked at the driveway, and Tom's car wasn't there. She nodded and smiled to herself. The first thing had worked out well. She paused at the front door for a few seconds. She pulled down her top to reveal more cleavage. Knowing what she had planned, she had gone for a tight short skirt for the job. She finally knocked on the door and waited patiently to hear the footsteps approaching. The doorknob turned, and she let out the last breath of doubt.

"Yeah, who's that?" Bobby said as he opened the door. "Oh!" He was taken aback when he saw Meeka standing in front of him. "What are you doing here?" he enquired as he looked around as though he suspected she had come to his house with an army that was still hiding behind his flowers.

"I was coming to meet Tom, but I don't see his car out front here again. He told me that he was here," she replied.

"Oh. Yeah, Tom was here, but he left. He said you wanted to meet up, so he went home," Bobby said.

"I thought he asked me to come meet him here at your house," Meeka commented offhandedly and shook her head. She looked towards the road where the taxi had been when she was walking to the front door.

"You can call him, so you know where he is," Bobby offered.

"Sure," Meeka said. "Do you think maybe I can come in for a while. I will really appreciate if I can use your toilet for a minute."

Bobby exhaled. "Yeah, sure. Come on in," he stood back and opened the door for her to walk in. "The toilet is just –"

"Don't worry, I know where the toilet is," she replied giving him a knowing look. She walked up to his bedroom and returned some minutes later. "I called him already. He said I should just wait for him here. He would come pick me up."

"Okay. That's great then," Bobby said. His eyes kept roaming around the room trying not to look at her or the way she sat on his chair.

"You know, you were really generous at that fundraising the other day. Giving up fifteen million dollars in just one single night – you're really the bomb Bobby."

"Thank you," he murmured and kept quiet again. When he couldn't take it any longer, he spoke up. "I'm sorry about the way Satin behaved to you that night. She already had too much to drink. She saw me with another girl earlier in the afternoon, and you know how she is," he shrugged.

"I understand Bobby; she kinda loses it sometimes. It's really nothing. I didn't count her threats to mean much," Meeka answered.

"Well ---" Bobby's eyes rolled around again. "Thanks for understanding."

"You're welcome Bobby," she replied. "You should already know by now that no one is gonna understand you better than I do Bobby. I mean, Satin's a really great girl, and I'm sure she knows just how much of a perfect guy you are. It's just that she doesn't get it. You know, she does not understand that desire – what pushes you to do what you need to do."

Bobby stared at her with a waring gaze for a second. "Why did you do it?" he asked.

"Uhh, do what?" Meeka looked at him, confused.

"Why didn't you use the condom as you promised me after I told you I was out," Bobby said.

Meeka paused before answering. "It was the heat of the moment, Bobby. We were both desperate to fuck that afternoon, and I just forgot."

"But you went to the bathroom."

"Yeah, I was going to wear it, but then I got carried away – I don't know how it happened, but all I could think of was to come fuck you, so I just turned back and came into the room." She kept a straight face as she dished the lies to him.

"It was going to be a perfect afternoon of sex, but then I went in, and I could feel your skin on mine – that was a mood breaker," Bobby said.

"I know, and I'm sorry about it," Meeka said. "I didn't mean to make things between us go sideways." She was now sitting straight forward, her legs spread wide open showing a better part of her laps.

"It's quite alright Michelle," he said and smiled at her. "Tommy's gonna treat you right I know that for sure."

Meeka scoffed. "No one's ever gonna be like you, Bobby. You're the best I've ever had, and I still want you."

"Now come on Michelle. You know that can't happen – it won't make any sense," Bobby answered.

Meeka stood up and sat next to him. "Who's saying that? Tom fucking knows it's only a matter of time before I come back to you, and I'm sure you don't really want Imani as much as you want me, so it's all about how badly do you want me. I want you Bobby, and I can have you right now." She raised her head to meet his lips, but he pulled away.

"Let's not do this," he said and shook his head.

Meeka pressed harder into him on the chair till he couldn't move back any longer. "You know you want this Bobby." She let her lips find their way to his mouth again, and this time he let her kiss him. The kiss lingered for about ten seconds before he pulled away again.

He pushed her back and stood up. "Tom will be here any minute. You should go with him and be with him."

Meeka was not going to relent. She stood up with him and wound her arms around his neck. "I want to be with you Bobby, not Tommy. You are the one I want, and I can see the look in your eyes, Bobby – you want me too. You really want me so don't hold back. You can have me right now." She gazed into his eyes, her pupils carrying a sensuous impulse he couldn't resist. As she raised her head up to him again, he met her halfway and kissed her. Meeka smiled in between the kiss and slowly directed him back to the chair where she sat on his laps and kept kissing him. Her hands soon found their way to his trouser as she rubbed his groin.

"I don't have any condom in here. I will have to get one from my car," he murmured and was pushing her off his laps, but Meeka held on.

"Don't worry about that Bobby. Let me see what your pull out game looks like. If you're coming just tell me and if you can't take it out, I'll pull away," Meeka said and gave him her seductive teeth smile.

Bobby sighed. "Okay." He returned to the seat and Meeka resumed stroking his penis through his trouser till his hard-on could no longer remain hidden. She helped him out as she kept kissing him. When she finally broke the kiss again, she inched herself up from his lap to drag off her panties and dropped it on the floor. She kissed him again and smiled. She massaged his stiff rod with her hand before standing up again, but this time as she made to sit back down, she helped his dick go straight into her. She adjusted her position on him before she began the vertical dance on him.

"Did you just learn how to do this?" Bobby gurgled the words out of his mouth, and he rested his back and let Meeka do all the work.

"I didn't just learn it, but we haven't done it before," she replied. Her legs were bent backward with her laps sitting comfortably half way on Bobby's lap and the remaining half on her bent leg. She held her balance in place with her palms behind her, resting on Bobby's knees so that she was leaning backward. She shifted her hips forward and backward, her weight keeping Bobby's dick perpendicular to her honey pot. "You feel like you haven't done it in a while," Meeka said as she kept rubbing the inside of her.

Bobby shrugged for a moment. "Kinda," he said. "Satin doesn't look like she is interested in fucking these days, and I'm not really feeling those other girls, so I've been on a low key," he said after thinking about it for a while.

Meeka shook her head as her breathing was now coming at a faster pace. "Well, you can change that." She removed her hands from his knees and placed them on his shoulder as she kept riding him hard. With her new position, she could kiss him while she made love to him. Bobby took her lips in and savored the wanting taste it carried.

"You should do this to me more often," Bobby said when he broke the kiss to catch his breath. "It is so fucking amazi – ama – ohhh – amazing!" he stammered.

Meeka smiled but said nothing. She held on tighter to his neck and raised her buttocks a few inches higher than they were before. At the same time, she began to let out the soft chime that always escaped her mouth whenever she was close to cum. "Stay with me Bobby," she pleaded as she rode him faster trying to sync their cum. "I feel you inside me, Bobby – fill me please." She raised her face to the skies as her climax rode out of the heavens. She had also felt the liquid shoot up into her – just as she wanted. For the first few seconds, Bobby had no idea what had just happened. It was until the excitement in him had died down he realized that he had cum inside her. He wanted to push her off his laps, but Meeka held on to him.

"Be fucking calm, Bobby. You needed it, so I let you do it – I'll just use an after-morning pill or something. You've got nothing to worry about," Meeka said. She climbed off his laps and pulled her skirt and underwear back up.

"Are you sure?" he inquired.

"Yeah. I'm sure," she answered and went back to sit down. She sat there for a while watching him bite his lips as he would always do when he was thinking about something. "I will say you make your decision before Tommy gets here," she said. "If he left when you said he did, then he would be here in less than five."

Bobby raised his eyes and stared at her unspeaking. "Let's do this shit," he said and sighed. "You know how to convince a man to get what you want," he added.

"Like you won't be getting what you want too?" Meeka laughed and walked to sit on his lap. "We'll be okay Bobby and don't worry; I'm going to break things off with Tommy once he arrives." She stood up and ran upstairs to his room. When she came back down, Tommy had arrived.

"I thought we agreed we should meet at my place? I was fucking racing down there," he lamented as he stood up. "You okay? You sounded really worried when you called earlier."

"Yeah. I had an issue I wanted to discuss with you then, but I am fine now," Meeka said and smiled at him. "But you know, there's still something I think we should talk about."

"Okay. What's that?" He walked back to take his seat as Meeka began to talk.

"You're a really good guy Tommy, and I kinda like you too, but you know this thing between us isn't real."

"Yeah. I kinda figured that out when you wouldn't stop whispering Bobby while we were at it."

"What I'm saying is I don't want you to miss out on other girls who will really like you just because of me. I think we should call things off." She sat down next to Bobby as she spoke to him.

"Okay. If that's what you want," he answered.

"That's what I want. Yeah," she replied. "Thanks for not making a fuss over this," she added.

"Why would I? I understood that we were just fucking – nothing else – nothing much," Tommy said. "So you guys are like back together uh?" he gestured at them with his nodding head.

"We are. It just happened. We had a talk and realized it was best we were together," Meeka answered.

"You both are good for each other," Tommy commented. He stood up again and patted his thigh "I should be on my way now so I can let you catch up with what's being going in each other's life while you were apart."

"See you later man," Bobby stood up and clasped the man's hand. "That went well," he commented after Tommy had left the room.

"I told you that he understood we were just fucking buddies."

"But really Meeka, how do you feel about going exclusively with me, then him and now back to me."

"It doesn't mean a thing, Bobby. Moreover, I wasn't exclusive with Tommy. I fucked other dudes you know," she replied.

"As if that isn't typical," Bobby raised his eyes at her.

"You're so gonna pay for that." Meeka stood up and sat on his laps. She covered his mouth with hers and her lips dissolved in the heat of the kiss.

8

Meeka and Bobby had started going out again for a little over a month. When Bobby broke things off with Satin the second time, she had been there to watch so she could mock her rival. She had walked the house all smiles, but as soon as she had sighted Meeka sitting on the couch, her countenance changed.

"What the hell is this bitch doing here?" she had yelled out and was already advancing towards her when Bobby popped his head out from his room upstairs.

"You're gonna let her be Satin," his voice rang out all the way from the top. He dragged himself downstairs where Satin was standing next to Meeka fuming with red-hot anger. "Satin, come over here," he called to her, but she remains affixed to one spot.

"If you've got something to say to me then I'll just stay here and hear you say it. I ain't moving an inch away from here," she replied.

"Okay. If that's what you want." Bobby took his seat. "We have to take a break from each other. It looks like you're not interested in me any longer and it isn't working for me anymore," he said looking straight into her eyes as he spoke.

Even though it was something she had expected, Satin still couldn't keep the hurt from showing on her face. She dropped a tear or two before cleaning her face with the back of her hand. "So she's the one who's gonna do it for you now uh?" she poked.

"She's here Satin, and she is definitely interested in me – you know, she does not treat me like shit at times and then take me seriously the next."

"I wish you good luck then, but I know very soon you're gonna be back begging me to bring my ass back to your bed." She turned to Meeka and wanted to talk, but she closed her mouth deciding against it. She pointed her finger at her as she shook her head before walking away.

"And that went better than mine," Meeka teased after Satin banged the door on her way out.

All that had happened over a month ago but just last night things changed – just the way she wanted it. Meeka was on the bed thinking about how she was going to bring up the topic. Bobby walked out of the bathroom, his body dripping as he picked up the towel from the bed. He went to stand in front of the dressing mirror that was standing from the floor to the roof. Meeka watched him as he soon began to hum Fat Joe and Remy Ma's *All the Way Up.* He was soon wiggling his waist as he sang the song.

"Bobby, can I talk to you for a minute," she started out. She played with her nails to distract herself from how serious and tense the atmosphere was soon going to be.

"Yeah, sure," Bobby answered and faced her. "What is it?" he asked.

Meeka saw no reason to beat around the bush, so she let the bomb drop immediately. "I'm pregnant," she revealed.

The smile she saw on Bobby's face looked like he was really happy at first but then few seconds into it, the smile turned into laughter, and soon he was rocking hard with laughter. "You're joking, right? You're just trying to mess with me – maybe you have a camera hidden away somewhere. Where's it?" he walked around the corner of the room searching if she could have a camera hidden.

"I'm for real Bobby. I'm pregnant. I took a test yesterday night, and it was positive," she said.

"This shit is for real Michelle?" he asked, looking a bit more serious now.

"Yes. I'm being serious here," she replied.

"How can that be? I've always been using protection."

"Yeah, I know – apart from that one time that we both didn't have any with us," Meeka said.

"But you fucking told me you were to going to take a pill or something. Didn't you fucking take the pill?"

"Don't yell at me, Bobby. I took the fucking pill, but I guess it didn't work."

"If you took the pill, how wouldn't it work? I fucking told you to let me get a condom from the car that day, but you just wouldn't listen – all you were concerned about was getting fucked." Bobby spat his anger around the room.

"And you didn't get fucked too? Come on. Don't make this all about me. We're both responsible for this."

"What are we gonna do about it then? This shit is really confusing me – what the fuck has been happening these past few days?!" he yelled out again and buried his face in his hand.

Meeka looked at him puzzled. "What the fuck are you talking about Bobby? I'm just telling you about the pregnancy now; I'm sure it isn't what's been making the past few days hell for you." Bobby remained quiet. "Just fucking talk to me. What happened that you haven't told me about?" She crawled to the foot of the bed where he was sitting and hugged him from behind.

Bobby raised his head up and shook it; his eyes had changed color within the few seconds. "What happened, Bobby? Tell me," Meeka pressed.

He exhaled and sighed at the same time and nodded his head. "Satin came to see me two days ago," he started. "She said that she was pregnant and it's mine."

Meeka's hand crawled out from his side, and she went back to hug the pillow she was resting on. "How sure are you that it's yours?"

"I could also ask you the same thing Meeka. Before I fucked you when was the last time you and Tommy did it? The day before? Two days before? How sure are you that it's mine?"

"I'm a woman Bobby, and I would fucking know if this is not yours," she yelled back.

"I'm not a woman, and I don't know so sorry that I still don't believe you."

"Tommy and I had sex just the first week we were together. I was not really into him after that, and that was why he was running to meet up with me when I called him the other time. He must have been thinking I was in the mood to get banged. I have calculated it, and this can only be your's, Bobby," Meeka pressed.

"Okay. If you say so. I'll take your word for it for now," he said and got up from the bed. "I've got to get to the gym now. We'll talk about this better when I get back." He quietly dressed up and eased out of the house.

The gym was a direct opposite of what he had left at home. It was all sweat, yells, cries, loud music and lots of comfy booties. Bobby walked over to where his training buddies were gathered training arms. They all hailed him as he joined in but didn't lose focus on their workout.

"Yo' gees. Wassup," he patted their backs and dropped his gym bag at a corner. He joined immediately and went into concentration curls. Thirty minutes later when they were mostly sapped out and dragging to get three reps of wide-grip curls done, Bobby brought up the topic.

"Guys, I need your advice on an issue," he said. "Shoot the big guy," Mac, one of his gym buddies said.

"Go for it Bobby," another said.

"Okay," Bobby agreed. "You guys still remember Satin right?" they nodded their head. "And you also know Meeka, the one I'm with now," they nodded their head again. "So I just found out that both of them are pregnant. Satin told me two days ago, and Meeka told me just this evening. I don't know what to do guys."

"Woah! That's one serious ish you've got there bro," Mac commented. "They can both be your baby mama though. You don't need to get serious with anyone of them if you don't want to."

"I know that Mac but I don't think it'll be good to have two kids away from their father. I was thinking if I should make an arrangement with one of them to stick around – but it can't be marriage. I can't get married to those girls," he said.

"You're fucked Bobby," Darrell said. He had been quiet all through the workout. "You could have just kept that dick of yours for one pussy, and you won't be in this mess. Or do you think those girls didn't know what they were doing before they let themselves get pregnant? They ain't novices at this game. They know how to make sure they never get pregnant, so if they are, they wanted it – and you know what that means to your cash man. You gotta take care of your blood."

"You think I didn't fucking know that before? Just keep quiet if you've got no solution to offer a brother," he spat out. He narrated how both of them happened to get pregnant.

"I would say you just pay them off – you know, a one-time settlement so you know you don't owe nobody and it's their choice to do with the money as they'd like," the crippling bald one amongst them, Hugo said.

"And if she wastes the money and my child suffers – what do I do then? I can't do that."

"Okay. What if you offer them both a settlement but you let them know you'll still pay child support. All you get in return is for them not to trouble you – ever. That is important Bobby. I know these girls, and they gonna suck you dry if you don't settle everything with them now," Darrell said.

"So what do I do?"

"What you do is fuck their brains out buddy – you know, you and the rest of your buddies," one of the trainers in the gym threw in as he walks by and laughed. "I'm just messing with you, Bobby. Just do whatever's best," he said and disappeared.

"That one's crazy," Mac commented.

"Well, he doesn't have the worst idea," Hugo said.

"How does fucking the two women pregnant with my baby solve the issue? I'll fuck them so great that they'll forget I'm gonna be their baby daddy? Be realistic Hugo."

"No. That's not what I'm saying," Hugo argued. "I was thinking more in the line of you, and some of your teammates should fuck both of them. Get the cash in the room – whatever amount the settlement is gonna be, bring it to the room, and everyone should fuck those two girls. Whichever one y'all can agree is the best, gets to take the money and will get the child support every month too. The other gets just child support. It's gonna be a win-win for you," Hugo said. "And before you say they won't go for it, I saw those girls at the fundraiser; they'll definitely go for it. They'll want to prove to each other that they're better so why not have fun while they do that."

"The sun did shine today!" Mac exclaimed, and the group burst into laughter. "But I've got to agree; he's got a great idea there. Just call me when you're drawing up a list of men that'll be in the room with you."

"I'll give it a thought guys," Bobby appreciated them. "I've got to run now though. A long drive back to the house." He said his goodnights and drove home with a calmer mind.

****

"I've thought deeply about this and what I've got may not be what you want, but it is just as good," Bobby spoke as Meeka and Satin sat in the living room, the hatred suffusing around the room, casting a shade on the light in there. "I'm not asking the both of you to become friends – I'm not gonna do that, but what I want is for the both of you to compete for two hundred and fifty grand cash."

"What the fuck did you just say?" Satin's interest was piqued already.

"Yeah. You heard me right. I will be giving two hundred and fifty thousand dollars to just one of you," Bobby repeated.

"And what do we have to do for it?" Meeka inquired.

"It's simple," Bobby replied. "You have both done it before, but this time it's gonna be with a larger crowd."

"You want us to fuck your buddies again?" Meeka asked.

"Yeah. That's the idea but this time around, the guys will decide who fucks the best, and that person will get the two hundred and fifty grand right there."

"Is that like a one-time payment or what? You're trying to avoid paying child support?"

"I'm not an asshole Satin. I'll take care of my child when the time comes – you both know that. The money is just to get you both off my neck."

"And the one who doesn't get chosen to be good at fucking?" Meeka asked.

"Well, you should be the one to ask," Satin mouthed.

9

"You said they should be here by seven pm. Where are they? It's already 7:09 pm," Doug grumbled.

"Yo Doug, calm down. They are just ten minutes late. It's not like you've been here all night," Mac countered.

"I've got things to take care of Mac, so if you don't know my business you just keep quiet over there," Doug retorted.

"So you mean like you've finally got something else to do aside from looking for a group fuck uh? Or maybe you haven't?" Mac replied.

"Guys, just chill out. We don't want any argument here. This isn't about any of you; it's about those two ladies. We're just a part of what they need for their competition. So the two of you need to keep your dicks in your pant at least till the girls get here," Tommy yelled at them.

Bobby was in the corner of the room. He and Martin were stacking the hundred and fifty dollar bills against the wall. The house they were using was one of Martin's hideout from his wife, where he brings his fleet of mistresses. They had met two of Martin's ladies in the house when they arrived earlier. The room was one of the new ones he just finished renovating. It had wall-sized flat screen TVs fixed on all panel, and the floor was well padded that it needed no mattress. The rapt knock on the door brought all of them to attention. Bobby nodded at Derrick who was closest to the door to check out who it was.

"It's them," Derrick announced as he pulled his head back into the room. Bobby gestured for him to let them in. "Hey girls," he greeted them. Meeka and Satin walked into the seventy by seventy feet room. They looked at the group of seven guys who hung around the room, the wait clearly written all over their faces.

"Hey guys," the two girls chorused and all the men did was smile at them. They smiled back. Bobby walked up to them. "Hey, how did the two of you get here together?"

"We met in front of the house," Meeka answered and looked towards Satin. She nodded.

"That's okay," Bobby said. "We're all set for both of you, just let us know when to start, and we will take it from there. Remember, this is

about how great you can please every one of us –
so you both should do your best." He looked on
from one to the other. "May the best woman
win," he said and walked away.

The two girls stood apart looking at the men, and
they prepared themselves for the game. They
walked over to the men with calculated
precision, their hips swaying with each step. The
seven men were all clustered. Meeka grabbed
Derrick by the neck and pulled his head down so
she could kiss. As her lips worked him, she
stretched her hands towards Jim, rubbing her
hand on his chest and slowly down to his groin
before tracing her path back to his chest and his
neck. Satin had taken on Mac. She had started
biting him on the neck and pushed her breast
against his chest as she went down on him.
Within ten minutes, both girls had all the men
with an erection under their shorts. They moved

back to glance at the marvel they had created. Their underwear soon came off, showing Meeka's supple dark breast with black rigid nipples that were standing close to a height of two inches. She had shaved her beneath that afternoon while she was preparing and it looked fresh under the bright white light that illuminated the room. Satin was a degree lighter in complexion than Meeka, her breasts were a bit smaller, but her nipples carried more width and had a shade of pink that looked like the wet nose of a white pig. She licked her thumb and dragged it along her skin down to her thighs, letting it linger on her clit for few seconds. Both girls walked back to the men and at that moment, the white light went off, rendering the room dark. All that was real to the seven guys was the padded sound of the feet walking towards them. Just as that sound stopped, the wall came to life, and the roof had a beam that cast a moonless night onto it. It sent a striking red lightning that stretched through all the four panels and then went dark again. When it came back to life, it was with a rumble, but it didn't stay long as the movie moved forward to the main event. The men were distracted by the screen, and the girls went to work. They peeled the men's underwear off their skin and took them through another ten minutes of unconsolidated pleasure. The moan of pleasure that soon began to escape the girl's throat could almost repress the moaning of the girls being banged in the porn video playing in the whole room. Bobby was hunched over Meeka, his fingers at the top of her clit as her head was in between his legs and her toes in his mouth. She pushed herself in and out as she also rubbed his testicles gently.

Two hours passed before the men were ready for their ritual. It had been a night of immense pleasure, and it was time to bring it to an end. Satin and Meeka were knelt down, their hands on their head and face raised upward while the men jerked the last block off their pipes, allowing their milky discharge flow onto both girls face and down their throat. They fell to the floor and remained there.

****

"So what are you gonna do with the cash?" Bobby asked her as she was dressing up.

"I don't know yet. Maybe I'll move upstate and spend a few years there before coming back to the city. I feel like I may need to detox a little bit," she answered.

"Okay. You take good care of our baby. I'll probably come see you a few times when we don't have to practice. I would have come with you but the season is starting," Bobby said.

"I know Bobby. I'll expect to see you soon though. You can have dinner and stay over," she said and smiled.

"I will," he answered. "And I will miss your smile too," he added before kissing her. He placed his hands on her protruded belly and kissed it. "Five months and I'll be a daddy," he smiled. "You be well Michelle," he kissed her one last time as she walked down the stairs and out the door into the waiting car. Bobby stood by the front door waving at her till the car disappeared.

THE END

71105473R00080

Made in the USA
Middletown, DE
20 April 2018